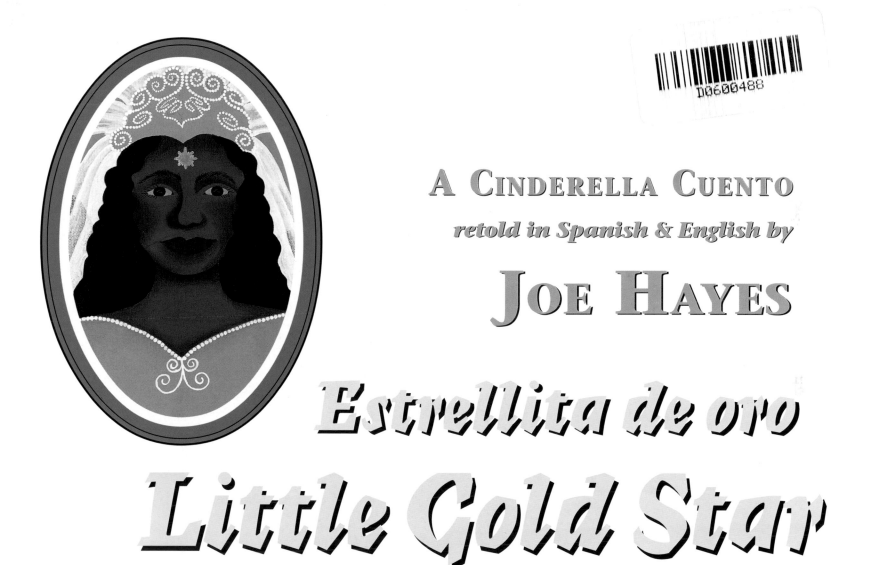

A CINDERELLA CUENTO

retold in Spanish & English by

JOE HAYES

Estrellita de oro

Little Gold Star

illustrated by GLORIA OSUNA PEREZ & LUCIA ANGELA PEREZ

❧ *For all the good stepmothers* —JOE HAYES
❧ *For my mother & my new family* —LUCIA ANGELA PEREZ

LONG, LONG AGO there lived a man whose wife had died. The only family he had was a daughter whose name was Arcía. The man's neighbor was a woman named Margarita, and her husband had died. Margarita had two daughters.

Every day when Arcía would walk down the street in front of Margarita's house, the neighbor would come out and give her something good to eat. She'd give her *pan dulce* or cookies or little honey cakes.

2

ACE MUCHOS, MUCHOS años vivía un hombre a quien se le había muerto la esposa. La única familia que le quedaba era una hija que se llamaba Arcía. La vecina del hombre era una mujer que se llamaba Margarita, y a ella se le había muerto el marido. Margarita tenía dos hijas.

Todos los días cuando Arcía caminaba por la calle frente a la casa de Margarita, la vecina salía para darle algo bueno de comer. Le daba pan dulce o galletas o pastelitos de miel.

3

One day Arcía said to her father, "Papá, why don't you marry our neighbor. She's very good to me. She gives me something sweet to eat almost every day."

Her father didn't want to do it. "You'll see, daughter," he said to Arcía—

"Today Margarita is so sweet and kind,
But her sweetness will turn bitter with time."

But Arcía insisted, "No! She's a nice woman, and you should marry her." Finally she got her way, and her father married their neighbor.

———— ⊂∩⊃ ————

Un día Arcía le dijo a su padre: —Papá, ¿por qué no te casas con la vecina? Ella es muy buena conmigo. Me da algo dulce de comer casi todos los días.

El padre no quería hacerlo.

Ya verás, mi hija —le dijo a Arcía:

Hoy Margarita muy dulce está,
Pero mañana Margarita se amargará.

Pero Arcía insistía: —¡No! Es muy simpática, y debes casarte con ella.

Al fin lo convenció y el padre se casó con la vecina.

At first everything was fine. But when summer came and the man went off to the mountains to take his sheep to the high meadows, the stepsisters started quarreling with Arcía.

Margarita no longer liked Arcía. She was very unkind to her. She bought many beautiful gifts for her own daughters—silken dresses and gold jewelry—but when Arcía's shoes wore out, she didn't even buy her a new pair. Arcía had to go around barefoot.

In time the bedroom was so full of the beautiful things of the stepsisters that there was no room for Arcía to sleep there. She had to move to the kitchen and sleep next to the stove.

Al principio todo andaba bien, pero cuando llegó el verano y el hombre se fue a la sierra a llevar los borregos a las praderas altas, las hermanastras empezaron a pelear con Arcía.

Margarita ya no quería a Arcía. Era muy mala con ella. Compraba muchos regalos hermosos para sus hijas—vestidos de seda y joyería de oro—pero cuando se le gastaron los zapatos a Arcía, ni siquiera le compró nuevos. Arcía tenía que andar descalza.

Con tiempo la recámara quedó tan llena de las cosas hermosas de las hermanastras que Arcía ya no tenía dónde dormir. Tuvo que cambiarse a la cocina y dormir junto al horno.

When Arcía's father returned from the mountains, he chose three young sheep from the flock. He gave one sheep to each girl. "Tend your sheep carefully," he told them. "When they're full grown, you can sell them and keep the money yourselves. Or, if you wish, I'll shear the sheep and you can spin and weave the wool."

The girls began tending their sheep, and Arcía took the best care of hers. Before long it was the fattest of the three and covered with thick wool.

One day Arcía said to her father, "Papá, I want you to shear my sheep for me. I'll spin the wool and weave it into a blanket to keep you warm when you go to the mountains."

8

uando el papá de Arcía volvió de la sierra escogió tres borreguitos de la manada. Le dio un borreguito a cada muchacha, diciéndoles: —Cuiden los borreguitos bien. Cuando hayan crecido, podrán venderlos y quedarse con el dinero. O si prefieren, yo los trasquilo y ustedes podrán hilar y tejer la lana.

Las muchachas comenzaron a cuidar los borreguitos, y Arcía cuidó mejor el suyo. Pronto era el más gordo de los tres y todo cubierto de lana espesa.

Un día Arcía le dijo a su padre: —Papá, quiero que trasquiles mi borreguito. Voy a hilar la lana y tejerte una frazada para que duermas abrigado cuando vayas a la sierra.

So the man sheared his daughter's sheep and Arcía carried the wool down to the river to wash it. She was bending over, washing the wool in the water of the stream, when suddenly a big hawk came swooping down from the sky and snatched it away from her.

Arcía called out to the bird, "Señor Hawk, please give my wool back to me."

And the hawk replied to her with human speech: "Lift…up… your eyes…. Look…where…I…fly-y-y."

So she did what the bird had told her to do. She turned her head and looked up. When she looked up, down from the sky came a little gold star, and it fastened itself to her forehead.

———— ✺ ————

Así que el hombre trasquiló el borreguito de su hija y Arcía llevó la lana al río para lavarla. Estaba agachada sobre el agua lavándola cuando un gran gavilán bajó repentinamente del cielo y le arrebató la lana.

Arcía le gritó al ave: —Señor Gavilán, devuélvame mi lanita, por favor.

Y el gavilán le respondió con voz humana: —Alza…la vista…. Mira…para…donde…vuelo.

Arcía obedeció al ave. Volteó la cabeza y miró para arriba. Cuando alzó la cabeza, cayó del cielo una estrellita de oro y se le pegó en la frente.

She went running home, and as she ran along, the wool fell into her arms, already washed and spun and woven into fine cloth.

When she got home Margarita said, "Take that piece of tin off your forehead!" And she grabbed her and tried to scrape the star off, but the more she scraped, the more brightly it shone.

Her stepsisters were filled with jealousy. They said, "Why shouldn't we have a star on our foreheads, too?" And they went looking for their stepfather to have him shear their sheep.

Fue corriendo a casa, y mientras corría, la lana cayó en sus brazos, ya lavada e hilada y hecha tela fina.

Cuando llegó a casa, Margarita le dijo: —Quítate esa hojalata de la frente. —Y la agarró y le raspó la frente para quitarle la estrella, pero entre más la raspaba, más fuerte brillaba la estrella.

Las hermanastras se volvieron locas de envidia. Decían: —¿Por qué no merecemos estrellas en la frente también?

Y se fueron a buscar a su padrastro para que les trasquilara sus borreguitos.

The first one found him and ordered him to shear her sheep. She went running to the river with the wool. As she was washing it in the water of the stream, the hawk came swooping down again and snatched it away.

"You evil bird!" she screamed. "Bring my wool back to me."

The hawk called down, "Lift...up...your...eyes.... Look...where...I...fly-y-y."

"What?" she said. "Don't tell me where to look. I'll look wherever I want to. Bring my wool back right now."

But finally she had to look up to see where the hawk had gone. When she did look up, down from the sky came a long floppy donkey ear and fastened itself to her forehead!

The girl ran home crying. When her mother saw her she gasped, "Bring me my scissors!" She took her scissors and snipped off the donkey ear, but a longer and floppier one grew in its place.

From that day on, everyone in the village called the girl *Donkey Ear!*

La primera lo halló, y le mandó trasquilar su borreguito. Fue corriendo al río con la lana. Cuando la estaba lavando en el agua, el gavilán bajó volando y se la arrebató.

—¡Gavilán malvado! —gritó—. Devuélveme mi lana.

De arriba el gavilán llamó: —Alza...la...vista.... Mira...para...donde...vuelo.

—¡Cómo que me dices dónde mirar! —dijo la muchacha—. Miro dónde me dé la gana. Devuélveme mi lana ahora mismo.

Pero al fin tuvo que alzar la vista para ver a donde se había ido el ave. Cuando miró para arriba, cayó una larga y floja oreja de burro que se le pegó en la frente.

La muchacha corrió llorando a casa. Cuando la vio, su mamá boqueó y dijo: —Tráeme mis tijeras.

Tomó las tijeras y le cortó la oreja de burro, pero en su lugar le creció otra, más larga y floja que la primera.

De aquel día en adelante, toda la gente del pueblo la llamaba *¡Oreja de Burro!*

But the other sister didn't know what had happened, and she went to the river with the wool from her sheep. She started to wash it in the water, and again the hawk swooped down and snatched it away.

"You rotten hawk," she shouted. "Bring my wool back."

"Lift…up…your…eyes…. Look…where… I…fly-y-y."

"I don't have to obey you. Bring my wool back this instant!"

But she too had to look up to find out where the hawk had gone. When she looked up, down from the sky came a long, green cow horn, and it stuck to her forehead.

She ran home, and when her mother saw her, she said, "Bring me a saw!"

With the saw she tried to cut the cow horn off, but the more she cut, the longer and greener it grew. From that day on, everyone in the village called her *Green Horn!*

Pero sin saber lo sucedido, la otra hermana fue al río con la lana de su borreguito. Se puso a lavarla y otra vez el gavilán bajó y se la arrebató.

—¡Gavilán asqueroso! —gritó—. Devuélveme mi lana.

—Alza…la…vista…. Mira…para…donde …vuelo.

—¡Cómo he de obedecerte a ti! Tráeme la lana en seguida.

Pero ella también tuvo que alzar la vista para ver a donde volaba el gavilán. Cuando miró hacia arriba, cayó del cielo un largo y verde cuerno de vaca que se le pegó en la frente.

Corrió a casa, y cuando su mamá la vio, dijo: —Trae el serrucho.

Con el serrucho trató de cortarle el cuerno, pero entre más lo cortaba, más largo y verde se ponía. De aquel día en adelante toda la gente la llamaba *¡Cuerno Verde!*

But all the villagers called Arcía *Little Gold Star*. And so Margarita wouldn't let Arcía go to town anymore. She made her stay home and do all the work. She had to cook supper and clean the house and wash the clothes. She had to chop firewood and carry water from the well.

Pero a Arcía todos la llamaban *¡Estrellita de Oro!* Y por eso Margarita ya no la dejaba ir al pueblo. La hacía quedarse en la casa y hacer todo el trabajo. Tenía que cocinar y limpiar la casa y lavar la ropa. Tenía que rajar leña y traer agua de la noria.

And then one day when Arcía was going to the well with her bucket, a messenger from the king's palace came by. He was spreading the word that the prince had decided he would like to get married. Since he couldn't find any girl in his own village to fall in love with, he thought he'd give a big party. Every girl from every village throughout the mountains was invited so that the prince could find a bride.

Arcía told her stepsisters what she had heard, and when the day of the party arrived, she helped them get dressed in their silken gowns. She fixed their hair for them so that it would hide the horrible things on their foreheads. She went to the door and waved goodbye as they went off to the party. She didn't even have a pair of shoes, much less a fancy dress for a party, so she had to stay home.

Y luego un día cuando Arcía iba a la noria con la cubeta, un mensajero del palacio del rey pasó por ahí. Iba pregonando la noticia que el príncipe se había determinado a casarse. Como no hallaba a ninguna muchacha de su pueblo de quien se pudiera enamorar, propuso hacer una gran fiesta. Todas las jóvenes de todas las poblaciones de la sierra quedaron invitadas, para que el príncipe pudiera encontrar una novia.

Arcía les contó a las hermanastras lo que había oído, y cuando el día de la fiesta llegó, las ayudó a vestirse en sus vestidos de seda. Les arregló el cabello para ocultar las cosas tan horribles que tenían en la frente. Fue a la puerta y las despidió con un adiós de la mano cuando se fueron para la fiesta. Arcía ni siquiera tenía zapatos, mucho menos un vestido bonito para una fiesta, y tenía que quedarse en casa.

ut that evening, all by herself at home, she began to feel sad. She thought, *It won't do any harm if I just go to the palace and look in the window to see what a fine party is like.*

She went to the palace and crept up to the window and peeked in. When she peeked through the window, the little gold star on her forehead began to shine more brightly than the sun. Everyone turned to look.

The prince called out, "Have the girl with the gold star come in here!" And his servants went running to bring Arcía into the party. But when Arcía saw the servants, she was frightened and ran home.

ero esa tarde, tan solita en casa, se puso triste. Pensó: "No hago ningún mal si voy al palacio para mirar por la ventana a ver cómo es una fiesta tan fina".

Fue al palacio y se acercó furtivamente a la ventana y miró adentro. Cuando se asomó por la ventana, la estrellita de oro en su frente empezó a brillar más fuerte que el sol. Todos se voltearon a ver.

El príncipe gritó: —Hagan entrar a la muchacha de la estrella de oro. Y los sirvientes corrieron a traer a Arcía a la fiesta. Pero cuando Arcía vio a los sirvientes, se asustó y corrió a casa.

The next day, the prince and his servants started going from house to house looking for the girl with the gold star. Finally they came to Arcía's house. But Margarita made her hide under the table in the kitchen and ordered her not to come out.

The woman called for her own daughters and presented them to the prince. "Your Majesty, one of these might be the girl you're looking for. Aren't they lovely young women?"

The prince took one look at the girls and gasped. He saw the cow horn and the donkey ear on their foreheads.

"No, señora," the prince said politely. "I don't think either one is the girl I'm looking for." And he started backing toward the door.

Al otro día el príncipe y sus sirvientes fueron de casa en casa buscando a la muchacha de la estrellita de oro. Al fin llegaron a la casa de Arcía. Pero Margarita hizo que Arcía se escondiera debajo de la mesa y le ordenó que no saliera.

La mujer llamó a sus hijas y las presentó al príncipe: —Su Majestad, puede que una de éstas sea la muchacha que usted busca. ¿Qué no son doncellas muy lindas?

El príncipe les echó un vistazo a las muchachas y tragó aire. Vio el cuerno de vaca y la oreja de burro que tenían en la frente.

—No, señora —dijo muy cortés—. No creo que ni la una ni la otra sea la muchacha que busco.

Y dio pasos para atrás hacia la puerta.

But just then the cat got up from her bed by the fireplace and walked toward the prince. The cat rubbed against the prince's ankle and purred, "Meeooow…meeooow… Arcía is hiding under the table."

"What was that?" the prince asked. "Did the cat say someone is under the table?"

"Oh, no," the woman said. "The cat's just hungry." She picked up the cat and threw it outside.

ero en eso el gato se levantó de su lecho junto a la chimenea y se acercó al príncipe. El gato se rozó contra el tobillo del príncipe y dijo: —Ñaauuu…ñaauuu… Arcía debajo de la mesa está.

—¿Qué es esto? —dijo el príncipe—. ¿Dice el gato que hay alguien debajo de la mesa?

—Oh, no —dijo la mujer—. Es que el gato tiene hambre no más.

Tomó al gato y lo echó afuera.

But the cat came right back and rubbed against the prince's other ankle. "Meeooow…meeooow…Arcía is hiding under the table."

"Yes!" the prince insisted. "The cat said someone is under the table. Who is it?" And he told his servants to find out.

When Arcía saw the servants coming toward her, she stood up. Even in her dirty, ragged old clothes she looked as fine and noble as a princess. The prince fell in love with her at first sight.

Pero el gato volvió en seguida y se rozó contra el otro tobillo del príncipe—. Ñaauuu…ñaauuu…Arcía debajo de la mesa está.

—Sí —insistió el príncipe—. El gato dice que hay alguien debajo de la mesa. ¿Quién es?

Y mandó a sus sirvientes a que averiguaran.

Cuando Arcía vio acercarse a los sirvientes, se puso de pie. Hasta con su ropa sucia y harapienta se veía tan fina y majestuosa como una princesa. El príncipe se enamoró de ella a primera vista.

The prince asked Arcía to marry him, and she said she would. A few days later, the wedding celebration began. It lasted for nine days and nine nights, and the last day was better than the first. And everyone was invited, even the mean Margarita and her two daughters—*Green Horn* and *Donkey Ear!*

El príncipe le pidió a Arcía que se casara con él, y ella le respondió que sí. A los pocos días empezó la fiesta de bodas. Duró nueve días y nueve noches, y el último día fue mejor que el primero. Todo el mundo fue invitado, hasta la envidiosa Margarita y sus hijas *¡Cuerno Verde!* y *¡Oreja de Burro!*

*I came on a colt
and I'll leave on its mother.
If you liked this story,
then tell me another!*

*Vine en una yegua
y me voy en el potro.
Si te gustó este cuento,
¡que me cuentes otro!*

Note for Readers and Storytellers

THIS CINDERELLA CUENTO was extremely popular in the mountain communities of New Mexico. All the traditional versions influenced my treatment of the tale, but I especially relied on that of Aurora Lucero White Lea in *Literary Folklore of the Hispanic Southwest*. It is from her version that I got the name Arcía. The traditional versions are consistent in many details and I've tried to retain what I see as essential to the story. The symbolic reward of a gold star on the forehead appears in almost every version of the Cinderella tale in New Mexico. It appears in other tales as well, but it seems especially central to this tale.

One way in which many traditional tellings differ from mine is that the animal which snatches the object away from the girls is most often a fish, rather than a bird. And in most versions the sheep is slaughtered and the sheep's intestines stolen, but I thought this detail was a bit gruesome for a fully illustrated picture book. Another element found in many traditional Hispanic tellings, but not in mine, is the appearance of the Blessed Virgin to advise the girls. Of course, only the heroine heeds her advice. I assume she is the same figure who is identified as the Fairy Godmother in the best-known version of Cinderella. I base my telling on a plot form that doesn't require her intervention.

As in my story, almost all traditional versions of the tale give the father's response to the daughter's request that he marry their neighbor in verse form, most commonly:

Si hoy nos da sopitas de miel
(Though she gives us bread pudding with honey today,)
Manana nos dará sopitas de hiel.
(Tomorrow she'll give us bread pudding with gall.)

This is a folk expression once fairly popular in New Mexico. The figurative meaning of *sopitas de miel* is roughly equivalent to the contemporary English expression, *nicey-nice*. And of course *sopitas de hiel* means the opposite. I changed the verse to one I learned from a teacher at the elementary school in Taos, New Mexico. The poetic elements of the Spanish make it more fun to say. But even more important to me is the name it provides for the stepmother. By referring to her as Margarita, rather than the stepmother, I was able to avoid something that causes some contemporary readers and listeners discomfort: the association of so many negative descriptors with the word stepmother in the old tales.

The little verse on the end of the story is more than decoration. Because the old cuentos date from a time when storytelling was a very important activity, they bear remnants of the rituals and formulas that accompanied the telling of tales. It was once customary to end each story with a brief verse, just as many people still end every prayer with the word *amen*.

—*JOE HAYES*

Visit **CINCO PUNTOS PRESS** at
www.cincopuntos.com
or call 1-800-566-9072

Spanish edit by Daniel Santacruz.
Cover design, book design, and typesetting by
Vicki Trego Hill of El Paso, Texas.

Hats off to Betty Brown and all librarians.
Thanks to Sharon Franco and Roberto "Beto" Perezdíaz for their help with the Spanish text. We'd like also to thank Beto—Gloria's husband and Lucia's father—for his support and friendship during the making of this book.
Thanks to Mariposa Publishing for permission to use "Little Gold Star."
Printed in Hong Kong by Morris Printing.

NATIONAL ENDOWMENT FOR THE ARTS

Funded in part by the National Endowment for the Arts.